The Hierarchy of Human Sufferings

A poetic anatomy of Grand Scale anguishes

Ernst Delma

Table of Contents

What is suffering?

Suffering is not quite the bread that lacks
It's the bitter bread one chews and swallows
Suffering is not the sugar one cannot afford
It's the sour sugar that swells the throat
Suffering is not the unavailable potable water
It's the tears that drown the soul
To make laugh those who cannot cry
Suffering is not the material miseries
It's the incurable diseases
Suffering is not the physical pain caused to others
It's the moral pain inflicted to oneself
It's the charity one concedes without generosity
It's the dollar given more by pity than by love
It's the loveless kiss on his wife's lips
It's the nonchalant arm on a friend's shoulder
It's the anguish caused to feel personal comfort
A bomb explodes in a café or on a plane
God cries Evil giggles, passersby are indifferent
Slashed flesh, crushed bones all over,
Blood scattered on the sidewalks or in the ether
The tongue that sows the venom of hatred
Instead of celebrating love and friendship
The arms that strangle instead of embracing
The teeth that bite in the flesh of others
The lips that lie and not proffering caring words
All that reminds God of His Creation's vanity
That is the Hierarchy of Human Sufferings
Suffering is killing God when slaying a Man

Introduction

This inquisition, modest by its sheer volume and perhaps in its persuasive ambitions, is centered on some of the greatest tragedies that have stamped Human History by the very magnitude of their severity. In fact, those events, that I must evoke in an attempt to illustrate what periodically puts our humanity on its knees, they are sadly famous. Their evocation, according to their impressiveness and the intensity with which they drew the world's attention, provides its title, The Hierarchy of Human Sufferings, to this exposé.

Why Hierarchy? They have not been of the same magnitude, and they have differently struck humankind in their physical and spiritual beings and in their consciousness. The world has much lamented of their occurrence. From the time of creation to these days, shedding tears and mourning has always been its share. It would not be an exaggeration to say that the human species has been suffering to its very viscera. From generation to generation, the heirs of perpetrators and victims of the human tragedy have passed down to posterity a heavy legacy, the indelible scars of the demoralizing episodes, natural or man-made, that have stamped humanity yesterday, stamp it today and will certainly stamp it tomorrow and forever. As long as there are minds to remember their acuity and history books to relate the severity of those difficult times that have visited us and probably will visit us, they will be remembered. The precise definition of history as being a perpetual occurrence is going to narrate that certain affinity for endless sufferings.

Striking tragedies, unbearable torments, have periodically been upon us to overwhelm us to an extreme we can barely endure. Their brevity and their degree of cruelty, measured by the damages they left in their wakes, have been ceaselessly astonishing. Their scars, indelible because profound, will remind us forever of their severity, and assessing them is revealed a useful endeavor in view to work toward their prevention or simply to limit the damages when their prevention only is another illusion of ours.

Concerning the testimonies and objections I call upon as illustrations, that they are my own reflections or have been quoted from others' works, sharing with this exposé a certain similarity, I hope that no part whatsoever is subjected to misinterpretation, taken personal or furnish matter to any sort of intellectual commotion. Accept as true, nevertheless, that its quintessence, although corrosive at certain points with respect to what it denounces does not aim at implying malice or causing conflicts in human relationships. Such an eventuality, I mean the unbiased evaluation of this inquest would be, in itself, worthy of enchantment.

In our direct or remote relationship, we do experience the propensity to use harsh reprisals when our convictions and proceedings do not meet the adherence of individuals that we would like either to win to our causes or to take for granted. How we see others and how we react to life's grandest or vilest events grant us the opportunity to praise the genuine acts of civility, to correct the past wrongdoings, to deplore the repulsive occurrences and eradicate the unpleasant aftertastes. That those deplorable episodes emanate from natural calamities or of the pain-causing episodes crafted by our fellow men's imagination as a manner of provocation or of retaliation, they all remain matter to reflections that call upon our sagaciousness and our impartiality for their analysis, their understanding and their interpretation.

The human specie, in its entirety, has been unspeakably suffering from either the hard blows applied by nature itself or from our fellow men's strange sense of humor, every time they decide to draw each other's attention on some particular beliefs, political doctrines or personal agendas. The religious, the political, the ethnic and the social have been at the basis of our chronic animosities, disagreements, ill-humors and our venal doings.

No matter what has triggered any episode of humankind's sufferings, that it was of natural occurrence or fervently elaborated by our foes' morbid imagination, it deserves the required level of awareness, must be treated with the adequate degree of intellectual probity, and has to be interpreted in function of how tremendously it has stunned humankind with respect to the paroxysm of the correlated sufferings it brought about.

Let's keep in mind, nevertheless, that there is only the hand that can erase the bad things to be capable of writing the good things. In other words, only the hands that can plow the land, can sow the flower-bed, water the blossomed buds and harvest the beautiful flowers. For an even more philosophical analogy, only those who are capable of forgiveness can write the most wonderful pages of Universal History.

We cannot neither run away from the ugliness of the past, nor assess the level of the forgiveness to consent by ignoring the wrongdoings and the incalculable human sufferings they spawned in our midst. On the contrary, we must face the hardships perpetrated on each other and have the courage to admit with Conrad"That they were done for us or against us, they were inadmissible". Our best excuses would be to deny them and to pretend that they were not committed by our actual generation; but, that would not change the rigor of the effected sufferings nor would, by some means, exonerate us.

Everything fashion of animosity that has contributed to give birth to the painful Hierarchy of Human Sufferings must be vehemently denounced in view to guarantee the definitive capitulation of humankind's adversities. They must be treated with the same intensity with which they have damaged our mutual pursuits of happiness as commanded by the Creator, guaranteed by conventions and penned as basic human rights by some of the handful benefactors of humanity.

Through the lines of this inquest, which is a swift ride across the immense field of human sufferings of which just few are surveyed, the advocacy for joining voices and forces to the reticent concert is patent. Being one of the self-proclaimed advocates of the salvage effort on behalf of the human experience, I present my apology to my fellow men on behalf of the perpetrators of all the debacles that have deeply mutilated us. From the first perpetrators Adam and Cain, to all the sinister figures that have slashed the Universe's profile with their bloody pursuits, they have just been the victim of poor education, wrong indoctrination and/or blatant disobedience to divine and human principles. Detailed analyses of some of the occurrences that have brought Human Sufferings to a nerves-cracking paroxysm constitute the background of this exposé.

Our world has been the scene of episodes at times so deplorable that they could bring the ones who got physically, morally or spiritually injured to regret their humanity. Don't the catastrophes strike so harshly every so often that one feels like uttering blasphemies against the

Divine One himself? Others often feel like expressing misleading assessments as, for example, those who have survived are too stubborn to wish to be still living and those who have perished did not deserve to live.

Sins, incurable diseases, famine, natural cataclysms, self-inflicted pains have been practically the underlying factors to human sufferings. Human endurance has often times been tested through them, and their strikes have been so severe at times that, in the wake of their manifestations, philosophers wonder about the reality of God's existence. Fredrick Nietzsche, for an example, and his Nihilism express doubt about God's existence.

Philosophers inquire around the reasons why the Divine One does insist so much in being conspicuously absent from the scene and let tribulations strike. Or, is it from him some sort of deliberate refusal of intervention, a strange sense of humor someone would say, to not alleviate the horrendous calamities that befall on humankind? We always expect swift answers from the Almighty; we want him to drop by as often as possible and to intervene as quickly as he can when our own equivocal demeanors launch us havoc.

The ultimate question worth asking, is God seldom or always responsible for every single one of the countless calamities that overwhelm humankind? Despite the dreadful biblical reminder according to which who strikes by the sword perishes by the sword or after having devastated you will be devastated in return, we still question God's hands upon all our sufferings. Or, if He was responsible, would it be a mean to give to sinners the opportunity to wash their sins through tears and teeth-grinding? Does our Creator provoke on purpose those unbearable anguishes so to command repentance for one's culpabilities? That would sound like a blasphemy against which Van Goth warns us***We cannot judge God by this world. We are simply a below par study of His*.**"

God has warned us and keeps warning us through the centuries about the irrevocability of his retaliation when we chose to ignore the imperativeness of his commandments. One of those philosophers, who still believe in the permanence of his ordinances, reminds us: "God does not have to intervene to punish the perjury the wicked ones carry in themselves the seeds of their own destruction".

As we enter the heart of the subject, as it occurs the analysis of some extreme episodes of sufferings-provoking, including birth – I would like to submit to your scrutiny this extract from Francis Lalanne's "Ballad to our Native God translated from the French. I am a bit reluctant to see essentially blasphemy in it. If it was the case, I would personally refuse to adhere to its paraphrase or its reproduction?

He appears to me rather blaming humankind for having spoiled the genuineness of our belief in the Supreme Being. I further decline to think that the singer-poet is upset at God, as no one has the authority to question God's ways and/or means; but, he bears a grudge against the terrestrial principalities, social institutions and religious authorities that have not been quite responsive to helping the enhancement of God's greatness. Those latter have rather been shining making him look petty, distant and a lesser God. On the account of our fellow Men's poor performance interceding on God's behalf, and the extreme anguishes to which humans are exposed, don't we have sometimes the tendency to believe that God has left his throne?

Ballad to our native God
Francis Lalanne

Listen Good God who lives in our midst,
Listen to the cry of the ones who suffer.
My hands stink like sulfur
For applauding in vain in the name
Of the one who turned water into wine.
It would cost you a bunch of annoyances
To change our misery in well-being
Before the end of Century Twentieth.
But, it hurts my ears and I can't sleep,
All those who cannot stop whining,
All the misfortunes no one dares to stem.

Listen God of heavens,
Listen the cry of the ones that cry

No matter what country and what time.
That they ignore or praise you
That dreadful misfortune has taken it all
Tears shed when blood sheds.
While up there you coo with a holy spirit
If you were truly a man
Come down and prove it to us.
You find it just people live on their knees
For an imbecile who robbed you of an apple?
Listen the cry of the ones who would like
That life be a baptism
And no longer an internment.
My heart is not beating to fight,
But even without a heart I will fight.
Tell me that you are not a bust of plaster
Like the one at the parish priest's house.

Good God of ours, this ballad,
If it could provoke your tears
Maybe I'd get some feedback from you
Good God of ours, this prayer,
Other than myself in their own way
Must have done it to provoke pity.
But I don't know how they pray you,
And I don't know how they write you
In the nations where you aren't the same.
But, if Men, far away from here,
Are your followers, them also,
Our prayers must be the same.

Then Good God in heavens

Good God of here or of elsewhere
If one day the world is better
Pray Men to forgive you
To have given them without asking you
This earth where you abandon them.

Birth, as source of suffering

A baby's first piercing scream, at birth, would be of terror. The great Leon Tolstoy intended – perhaps in vain – to convince us of the rationality of such an assertion; but, erroneous it still says for many. According to this statement, presumably already horrified to enter an unfair world, the baby would, thus, express discontent or fear. The innocent anticipation of the countless sufferings he is called upon to endure during the course of his terrestrial existence would bring the newborn to articulate such an early panic.

Does Tolstoy's above-mentioned assertion suggest that the baby, since her mother's womb, has somehow been aware that – in agreement with Jean-Paul Sartre - "hell is the others". The baby's bawl right at his entrance in life, an innate reflex according to Tolstoy's theory, suggests a premonition around the enormity of his sufferings to come already in confection somewhere in the vast world.

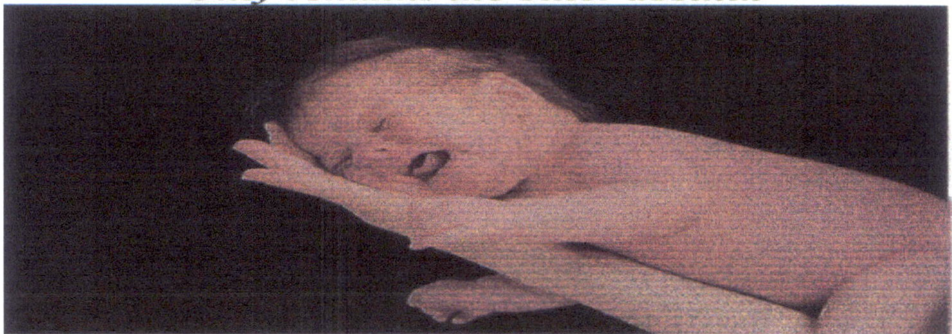

The overwhelming hierarchy of human sufferings can hardly wait to integrate the new born in a vast routine of inevitable miseries lurking, way before birth, in the anguish-making indentations of life and aiming at striking all along destiny, no matter someone's race, background or degree of fame, of importance or of riches. All differences are reconcilable in the eyes of terrestrial calamities. Before God, we are all equal amid sufferings, as we are in death.

Although a scientific explanation would appear more convincing, yet isn't there a good reason to believe, in point of fact, that the baby was warned, except that the choice to come or not was not up to him, but to their progenitors' will. We solely have to arrive into existence against all odds and the Hierarchy of Sufferings triggers the awful mechanisms of individual and collective anguishes. The famous Haitian poet Coriolan Ardouin once lamented on the course of the misfortunes that have afflicted his existence from birth to his premature death.

You have rejected my birth, Oh Providence,
Since a black butterfly[1], the day of my birth
Landed on my cradle. Oh, I so suffered since.
I lived, sleepless and tearful, so many nights
Since, at twenty, I beheld my parents' passing
The honey ran dry, only remains bitter absinth

Coriolan Ardouin, the first true romantic poet of the Haitian literature, had indeed suffered up to his death at the young age of 23. The death sentence has been pronounced at birth, and since then anguish, on one form or another, has been ceaselessly at his bedside, faithful to its duty, followed him as a vocation, a life's sentence, a stubborn bad luck, a hot iron collar.

Women, depositaries of sufferings.

« I will add suffering to your pregnancies. You will give birth in pain "(Genesis 3:16). It was the Creator's verdict towards Eve. Since then, her emulates live on their knees before the altar of

---

[1] In the Haitian mythology, a black butterfly sighted in the house is a sign of death lurking. Often people confess having spotted a large black butterfly either in a corner or on the house's wall prior to some beloved one's death.

suffering. Menstruation, loss of virginity, pregnancy, birth and their corollaries, you name it and women answer present to the call.

From giving birth to mourning lost ones, women seemed detaining the exclusivity of the matters of which sufferers are made. They do indeed achieve the palm leaf of sufferings with honor mention. Our mothers, our sisters, our wives are together the emblems of happiness and the sum of all unbearable sufferings. The image above, doesn't it corroborate with such an observation?

Yet every tear washes something and frees human conscience of the dirt of existence. Tears are like the blessed water that washes our souls from the debris of bitterness collected in our daily frictions with all terrestrial calamities, and all that prevent us from transcending beyond ourselves, including ourselves. We cannot rid ourselves of the carnal envelop that weighs down our transcendence amidst our most elevating excitements and good deeds without contemplating chaos. Aren't we, at times, the artisans of our own sufferings, the victims and the executioners, the wounds and the knifes of our aspirations to happiness?

The Faces of Distress

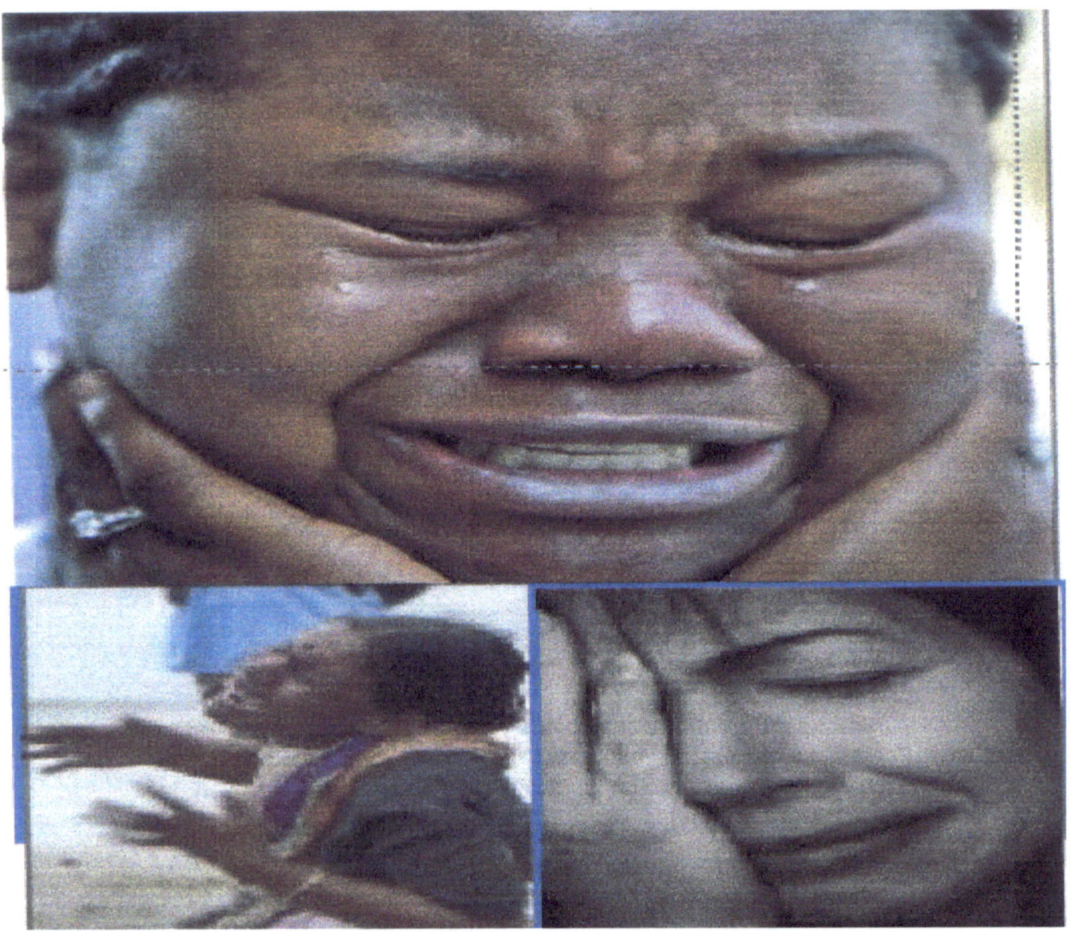

The Hierarchy of Human Sufferings   Ernst Delma

A pair of soggy eyes, tightly closed,
as opaque windows, on unfathomable misfortunes.
Tacit but eloquent expressions of all painful occurrences
That pave all boulevards that lead human species' existence
to bring their sufferings to the most lamentable paroxysm.
Bitter exteriorization of insurmountable calamities
that propels human morale beyond the edges of human fortitude.
What manner and what else is a better approach
to tell about the harshness of humankind's frequent sorrows?
If not by a pair of eyes resolutely fastened
On the terrifying advent of unutterable calamities.
Death, famine, murder, hand-crafted or mind-crafted miseries,
Unwanted trials that defy the dreadful sequence of command
That unleashes the Hierarchy of humankind's sufferings.
Eyes tightly closed help the souls absorb unforgiving harshness.

Ernst Delma

Men's tears

Do men cry? If they do, are their tears sincere?

Rumor has it that men do not cry as if born with a steely and a soul sealed against any sort of tenderness, of compassion, of altruism or any of those sentiments that bring a man to feel human. But a man with a heart to shed tears on his own misfortunes or a soul to partake others' misfortunes is a man of courage. Are courageous indeed, the men who can cry.

It just takes a breath of magnanimity and of fortitude for a man to be human enough to cry. Or, the object of demonstration of such a degree of humanity must be singular in its essence. It takes more wisdom to confess one's degree of humanity through tears more than any other criteria of evaluation.

A man who cries is a man lucky enough to experience noble or complacent feelings and exteriorize them through his wet eyes that it is in his moments of greatness as of those of weakness, in success as in failure. Certain men cry in the midst of unbelievable occurrences as they do amidst unbearable misfortunes.

A man, as long as he lives, cannot rule out the possibility of facing moments of undeniable success as of moments of deplorable failure. He constantly deals with two intermittent impostors – triumph and breakdown – that compel him to fall on his knees and weep, with dry eyes at times shedding tears abundantly. Men cry to eternize moments of great accomplishments, to mark the achievement of notable wisdom or to exteriorize the acuity of their unhappiness.

A simple but typical example, a man sees a dying indigent at the corner of some street, weeps and says "God bless your soul" and closes his eyes because he has a soul to share with others in their misfortunes, he is a blessed man. That is a blessed man showing wisdom in its most perfect manifestation.

Another man see an old woman dying and turns his face:" It's nothing, it's just another inevitable death occurrence: it's simply and old woman dying, why bother and lament about her fate?" He simply is another kind of man, a dry-hearted man who does not have a heart to dedicate to comprehension, to commiseration. He is indeed a pitiful man. This is the image of a man not touched by misfortunes, similar to a block of ice on which emotions fall and slip away. He is neither a superman, nor a better man, nor a bad man. He is simply a different man for not being able to share his soul through the tears of his eyes. When we don't shed tears, they stay in us, become stagnant, harden our hearts and internally corrupt us to the extreme.

Only God may gauge the degree of humility behind a man's tears or the oddity of his inability to respond to anguishing occurrences because God himself expresses through humans' eyes human feelings associated to life's unfortunate events. This concept explains the difference between manly reactions in moments of distress as in moments of joy as being in direct correlation with the presence and absence of moral and spiritual ferments, which sets free a specific response to those events we mentioned earlier.

Some Men do cry and, in each tear, radiates the fullness of the parcel of His divinity God placed in each of us at birth. Their hearts are like sponges that absorb the sum of all sufferings of existence. Aren't they fortunate because they can cry and indeed cry when needed considering that truly every tear washes something and alleviates the conscience? The eyes are the soul's windows not just to open on life, but also to drain through tears the moral and spiritual wastes that would otherwise stagnate and overwhelm human existence.

The ones who don't cry are not supermen, as one might incline to believe; they simply cannot cry. They are made of a difference substance. Their souls are like blocks of ice on which emotions and sensations fall and slip to the ground. Are they more fortunate, those who cannot cry? Certain life's events persuade to believe that one must let one's soul to wash itself with a great abundance of tears thus preventing spiritual and moral stagnations.

Being capable of crying is a human virtue that not everyone is given the opportunity to experience. Sensitiveness is in a class by itself, and men who can express it have been praised all along just for being able to do so, and they have indeed left their marks on humanity in a very special manner.

Insightfulness level with the skin, goodness level with the heart command the necessity of men's shedding ears, to cry and save humanity of the dehumanizing indifference that deprives existence of its dearest and worthiest intrinsic qualities.

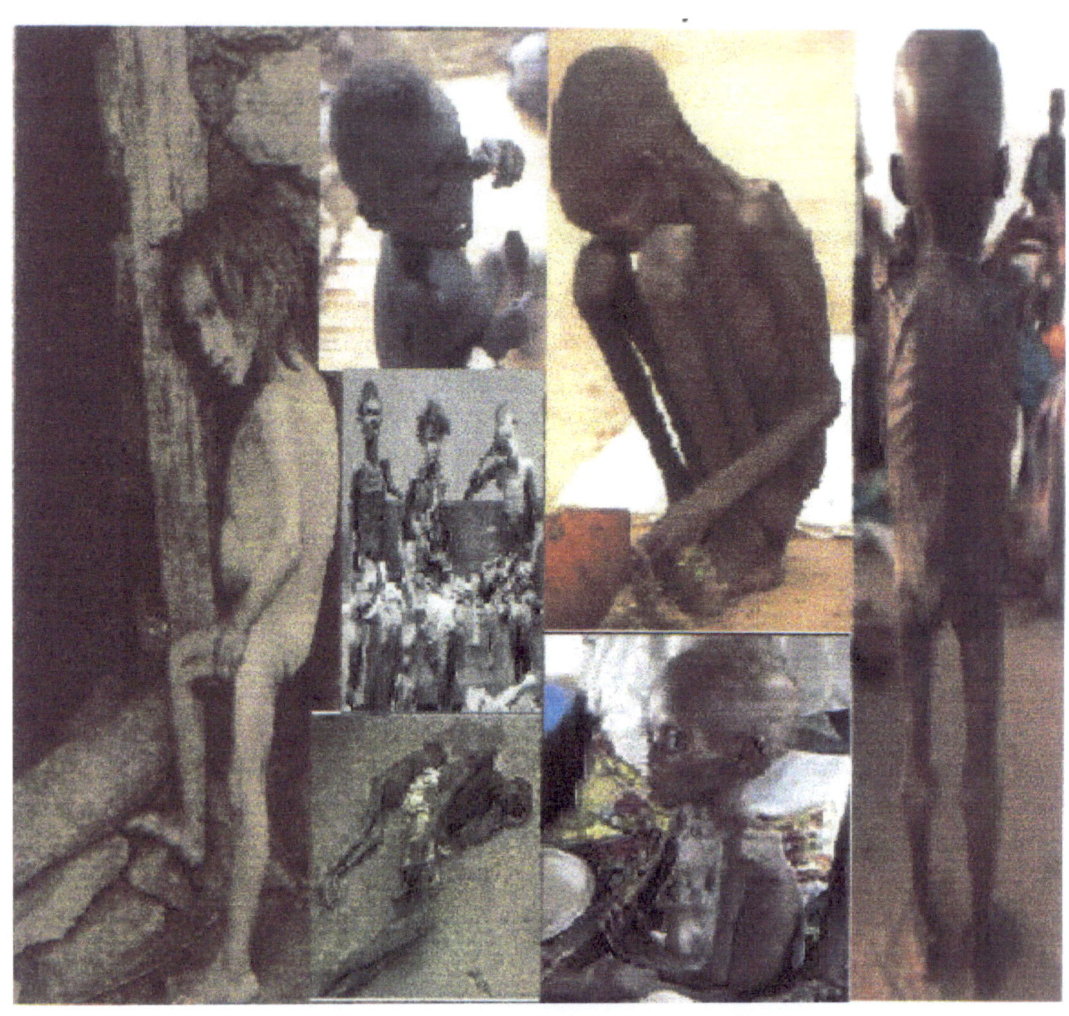

Those God's orphans, living skeletons, young, but ripened and aged by atrocious sufferings, hellish adolescence, they prematurely endure one of the most heart-rending peaks of the Hierarchy of Human Sufferings, famine.

Victims of the most revolting abuse humankind makes to humankind among them to let youth, the future of humanity dies of hunger or from some kind of disease, deprived of basic education, forgetting as the Ghanaian proverb puts it:" The fall of a nation begins in the houses of its citizens.", they physically, morally and spiritually decline since the adolescence stage and the future of a nation or of the world declines with them.

Three gains of corn, Mother
By Amelia Blanford Edwards

Give me three grains of corn, Mother
They will keep the little life I have
Till the coming of the morning.
I am dying of hunger and cold, Mother,
Dying of hunger and cold;
And half the agony of such a death
My lips have never told.
It has gnawed like a wolf at my heart, Mother,
A wolf that is fierce for blood;
All the livelong day, and the night beside,
Gnawing for lack of food.
I dreamed of bread in my sleep, Mother,
And the sight was heaven to see;
I awoke with an eager, famishing lip,
But you had no bread for me.
For bread to give to your starving boy,

When you were starving too?
What has poor Ireland done? That the world looks
sees us starve?
Quick, for I cannot see you, Mother,
My breath is almost gone; Mother! Dear Mother!
Ere I die, Three grains of corn.
Would give life to me and you.

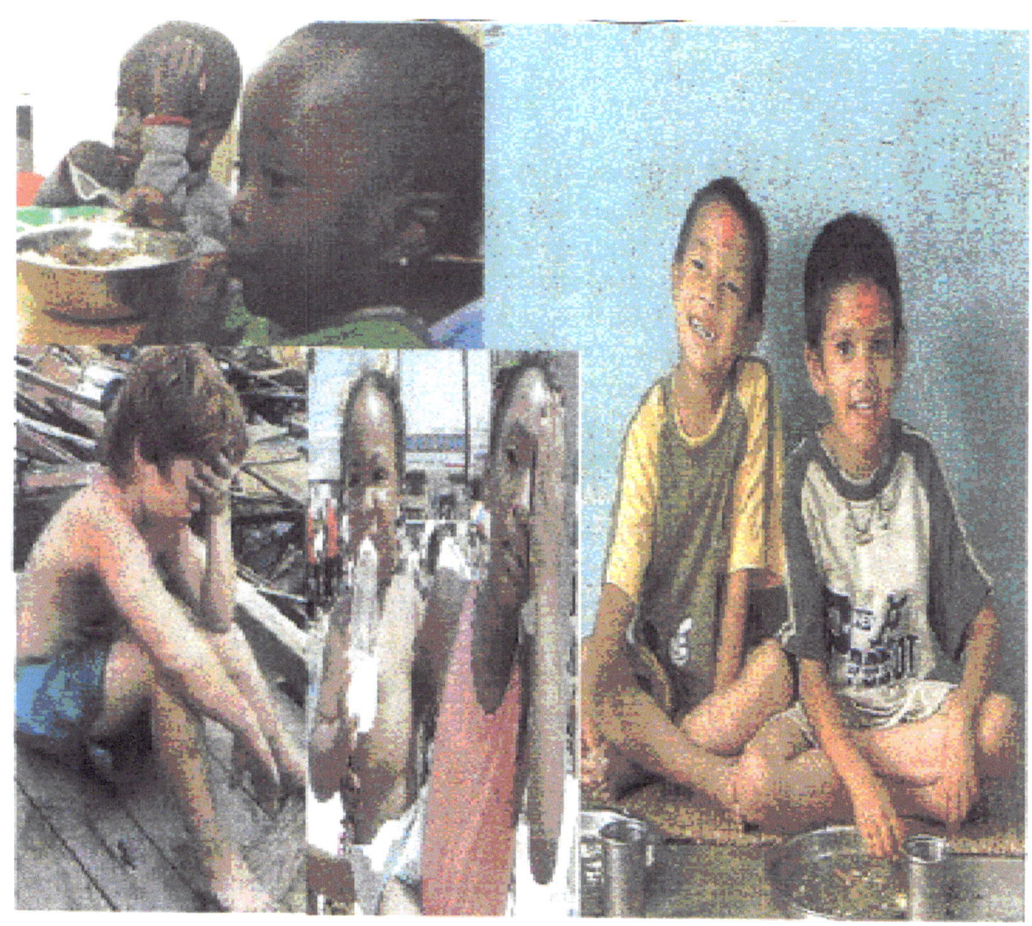

Little orphans, smiling amidst extreme miseries.
What stoicism you show that luckier ones are not capable of
Where do you get courage to smile?
Amidst such sufferings as those provoked
By famine and incurable diseases.

You daily giggle with death.
Thus giving a lesson to better-offs and to
Grown-ups.
What God has made you so courageous?
Is it innocence or premature heroism?
I see you as leaders and commanders
In route to a better world
Where find solace only the ones
Who know how to be stoic, to hope
And to love, despite all.

.

The little orphan's song

My parents left long for a remote shore,
One morning, despite my tears, they left.
Gone to thrive a while amongst others,
Promising to return with bread and toys.
I'm still waiting, as they're yet to arrive.
Hope is vanished, illusions are shattered.

Since my childhood, they left for the city
To search for better live or beg for pity.
But, got lost. My distress knows no pair.
I know they are someplace in big town
Serving dear children who can acquire
All up to other children's mothers.

I yearn death that rejects my supplication
To rid me of the hell of my deprivation
Life's roughness still withers up my soul
And absence of joy makes my life dull

The Hierarchy of Human Sufferings   Ernst
Delma

Whenever a frail joy caresses my face
It's to drop me in more intense disgrace.

Daily, I chew pain and digest bitterness,
I anticipate dejection, I chant loneliness.
Friend, let me use your carving scalpel
To one by one rid me of my vital cells.
My fathers are gone, why trying to thrive
Amidst such agonies,why keeping alive?

Harvest without a smile

The Hierarchy of Human Sufferings   Ernst
Delma

Not even a smile to welcome the grain pouring
That sparks a streak of hope for tiresome farming.
No exalting transports to greet the arrival of plenty,
Thankful rousing rather commands stoical indifference.
Hope so often and so steadily gangrened by despair
Makes the smile unreasonable amidst bountiful harvest.
Disbelief born from chronic unmet fulfillment
Represses the outburst of waves of contentment,
Cause any penchant for thrill is long gone, all delight buried,
Deeply covered under the mortar of obstinate denials,
Perplexity and confusion reign in conquering instructors,
As calamities and setbacks congest all the paths to exultation.
When constant tears, similar to acid rains, flood human confidence.
Only displays itself the gruesome specter of painful occurrences.
Today's laughter drowned in tomorrow's tears, lasting anguishes
Harden profiles; chill the warmth-radiating silhouettes of yesterdays.
Dead eyes with empty gazes reflecting crushed spirits become legacy,
No smile any longer to welcome the perspective of bountifulness,
Impassive postures henceforth greet the pouring of seeds.
The recurring advent of man-made calamities
Have atrophied all élan of fervor towards genuine pursuits,
And have achieved to tone down all burst for festive ecstasies.
The confused beneficiaries of the erratic efforts are too aware
That the gods of the lying Providence apart can at will tear
The fragile veil of joy and reappoint the mechanisms of tears
Turning the harvest basket in a vase of sorrows, bliss turns in fear.
They know too well that the foremen of the famine apocalypses,
Can at any moment trigger the apparatus of scarcity practice
To upset the world of eternal grain-pickers in uncertainty.
They've learned to sow and harvest in a posture of silent dignity.
Why smiling, the wicked forces behind the relentless déjà vu,
Are so faithful to their disparaging and disgraceful rendez-vous?

To reiterate my vow of absolute impartiality in my analysis of the occurrences - natural or man-made that I will have judged appropriate to the development of the inquisition – occurrences that have always baffled humanity because of the roughness with which they set in; I intend to make of the **poetry for peace** maxim the justification of this exposé. Thus, I would difficultly forgive myself if I have not chosen to share with you the profound content of a French song from Fancis Lalanne that I have - with the best of my ability – translated for you. I don't ambition to reach the neatness of the quintessence of the poem because as someone has opined in reference to texts translations:" *when they are beautiful, they are not faithful, when they are faithful, they are not beautiful*". Nevertheless, I simply anticipate the gratification of your forgiveness if it does not reflect one hundred percent the singer-poet's quintessential inspiration.

I absolutely agree with him that the most troubling and most regrettable episodes of the Hierarchy of Human Sufferings come from man-made calamities. Better than us humans, nature knows exactly when to loosen the garroting mechanism, not us. We always wish we could bring the anguishes of our fellow Men to an unbearable extreme. That reveals that God and Nature have more class than us. Could we, at least, agree that God and Nature have class in their torment making, and that we are rather pitiless?

In any case, let's sustain that Francis Lalanne is of the race of philosophers who think just like me — allow me this pretense — that the best way to prevent further animosities, calamities and sufferings is to have the courage to denounce past animosities, to scrape the fatalities laid at the foundation of the man by man miseries with a great deal of moral conviction. I hate to believe that such rightful and conscious moves might provoke the indigestion of the ones who think that the world is better off with its range of sufferings-making episodes. The idea of a totally peaceful planet simply does not meet the consent of some establishments, and the impression that such an eventuality is not unanimously desired would not be false if thought of and uttered.

Such a philosophy skirts resignation, intends to promote the idea that all is well and fair when all is not essentially bad or malicious.

The world is spiritually healthy when the world does not behave in disagreeable manners. There is no absolute true in such a debatable conviction. On the contrary, it's like Jean Racine, French playwright of the classic period, wrote in his Iphigenia:

"Since after so many efforts my resistance is useless
To the fate that drags me along, I indulge myself in blindness"

All is well is pure utopia, and all is bad is often an extreme conclusion. There is not just ugliness in the world, and the world cannot pretend either with a convincing fashion to any irreproachable performance. We must constantly patch, heal, limit the damages inflicted to us by us and with conscience manage the strange relationship that characterizes us. We just mutually intimidate each other with a constant war declaration with just short moments of relaxation.

Regrettably enough, I do not have the how propitious stage for, armed with a guitar and a voice, pleading human case, either presenting the human apology for the evil already done or preventing the happening of the malevolence that is about to be done; but armed with a pen – the mighty instrument of little men, as Lord Byron has put it. Through the following lyrics – lyrics that have always shaped my conviction towards the concept of peace - I claimed Mr. Lalanne's assistance to present humankind's apology before the totalitarian tribunal of unforgivingness.

I only wish the reader could believe how sincerely I hope that one day voices from the top and those from the bottom can strike in unison the melody of human harmony that friends in low places and friends in high places could blend their eloquences to pound, with authority, that it is time for all misfortunes to succumb. The world, our world, so far, has been trembling in its very foundation and the tremors have been catastrophic. Now, a reasonable wish would be that September 11 - or any similar episode - is only a nightmare that has been. In simpler words, no more.

Song for peace
From Fancis Lalanne
translated from French

I don't believe in the islands
Pain doesn't exist
I don't know any tranquil ones
I know some that carry misfortunes.

The wind that blows on the land
Carries the sob of the tides
Children died in Ireland
And their mothers have not cried.
Do you viler war
Than the one cynically baptized 'civil war'
Words have a sense to dig
Civil and polite are brother-words
But someone who is civil or soldier
Does one kill politely his brother?
Then I place my trust in Pravda.

I hear crying storks
Those bring us the newly-born
Brother kills his brother in Poland
Does Cain have Polish blood?
But the vilest of those wars
That in a same region
Can stand a son against his father
Are religious wars.
In the name of God to kill a man
Is to kill God himself
And what is then the hope of man

When man is a wolf for his God.

Bleed eternal snows
Poppy on white lily
I've seen the original stain
At the foot of a cedar in Lebanon.
Certainly beyond frontiers
Men bring death
But it is in foreign land
Is there more remorse?
Yet we are preparing one, which,
according to the words, can destroy even the moon
And make of the world a cross.

The vultures fly over the town
When war has made its choice
All wars are civil
'Cause death has no nationality.
See
Closer to us in Spain
Basks defy Bourbons
And home anger is winning
From Corsica to the Britain country.
Thus was born the end of earth
Before term as it is.
If others have chosen to keep quiet
But one must point to it
If others have chosen to tone it down
It belongs to you to denounce it
To you to point to it.

The wind that blows on the world

> Tell me what it brought you
> If it brought you suffering one day
> Don't be surprised.
>
> The wind that blows on France
> Blows, they pretend, in all freedom
> But beware of all appearances
> 'Cause one good day the wind might switch its direct
> Beware of all appearances
> 'Cause one good day,
> the wind might blow something else.

Before progressing to the full development of this subject — I hope it will sharpen the reader's interest — enjoined on me by all the might of its appropriateness as that of the yeast of potential divergences it holds, I would like to submit to your perspicacity a few verses I have composed, which relate — among many other things - the epic but fatal character of the human odyssey on earth.

The initiation of our terrestrial experience has been stamped, according to the biblical legend, by two facts, terrible in their nature, remarkable in their signification to us human beings. Those two facts are at the basis of all human sufferings endured by the Creation from the time of their perpetration to this very day. This is the typical example of how one man's misdeed constitutes the stumbling-block to his fellow men's existence or the prevention of all possible pursuits and enjoyment of total happiness on earth.

This development outlays the dilemma emanated from our first parents' disobedience – Eve having seduced Adam, having convinced him to bite in the forbidden fruit – and our big brother Cain's famous crime perpetrated by jealously on his younger brother Abel. Since those episodes our humanity has been haunted, it's been the relentless launching of a whole range of periodical misfortunes for the entire world to cope with, unavoidable, but untenable and at times formative, sufferings keep coming our way when least expected.

The hierarchy of all human sufferings is in direct correlation with the fundamental sin committed amidst the magnificent Eden Garden's. Adam has misbehaved in the midst of comfort created on his behalf, and since then we have not been faithful making of happiness on earth a tangible and definitive acquisition. Our endeavors to contemplate durable human felicity have been seesawing dreams that sufferings of some sorts, as a brutal awakening, destroy at each one of our attempts.

Adam has bitten into the apple despite God's ordinance to not do so, and God has swiftly and fiercely reacted against his disobedience. ***Thorns and also thistles shall it bring forth to thee.***" and further ***"You will earn your bread at the sweat of thy face."*** was the sentence. To Eve he said:" ***I will add suffering to***

your pregnancy, you will give birth amidst great pain. »

God's reaction to Adam's disobedience to his ordinance proves that struggling as a devil in a stoup to procure oneself the inaccessible does not always meet the divine one's adherence, can cause the collapse of the bridge between us and him, and can be fatal, to us, human beings, is so many different ways. And to sustain his verdict in the wake of any disobedience of ours, God has at his disposal a whole menu of options. The Great Flood, Sodom and Gomorra's consumption, the fall of Babylon, the taking of Jericho are all perfect biblical illustrations of how harsh God's retaliation can get.

Cain has killed his brother Abel and God has pronounced the ultimate sentence, which in turns proves us that God hardly forgives or will never forgive us bloodshed not even in his name and for any alleged reason whatsoever. He severely punished indeed such execrable way to settle our animosities or to reconcile our differences, whatever the motives at their basis might be.

He questioned Cain:" What have you done? The voice of your brother's blood cries unto me from the ground" Genesis 4:10 and further:" A fugitive and a vagabond you shall be on earth" Cain to reply:" My punishment is greater than I can bear." Genesis 4:13.

Since then, it has been the faithful unrolling of human sufferings. The following verses of mine illustrate so well how expensively humankind in its entirety has been paying in homicide and bloodshed for the very first horrible fratricide known to humans.

Since Cain and Abel…a craving for blood

Since the first fresh cup, still smoking, handed by Cain
In the wake of his brutal killing of his brother Abel,
The devil, struck by the warmth and aroma of the vile beverage,
Keeps asking relentlessly more and more.
The red liquid, the fatal drink, having enchanted
The devilish prince, the sentence was since then pronounced.
Thus, at each fatal crossroad of human history,
At each resurgence of a new political pulsation,
Each acrobatic twist of universal thought
Brings about a new wave of crime against humanity.
It solely takes the self-sufficient attitude of an eminent brute,
A handful of rejoicing supporters to assent to his follies,
A thousand of wild devotees to excitedly give a standing ovation,
Another imminent danger glides its tenebrous veil on the horizon,
And the world suddenly becomes the stage of another carnage.
Another fatal road encouraging unspeakable rage
Has been crossed and the written frontispiece of men's slaughter
Is dressed where the modern Cain(s), faithful to the contract,
Are about to be given a new chance to feed the cunning prince
With their brothers' flesh and blood.
Since then, it's been the eternal misfortune, the false logic
Of Cham's children paying their fathers' curse
To an endless fourth generation.

The Hierarchy of Human Sufferings   Ernst Delma

Since then, it's been the tyrant and the oppressed.
The pitiless wars for conquests and subdues
Where the great and the iron-hearted lead the terrorist cavalry
At the expense of the humble and of innocent lives.
The terrible ones, miserable figures of misery-making,
Fervent experts in all wakes of human disquietude,
Romantic vagabonds dressed with sinister garments,
On horseback, scattering terror amidst widows and orphans.
Blood-thirsty Attilas, wild Alexanders, intrepid Shaka Zulus
Cannibal Hannibals, demented Caesars and refined barbarians,
Decked generals, solemn in silks and leather boots
Racing the world in their sinister rallies of death,
Followed by fortified tanks spoiling the exuberance of fertile hills.
Blood-shedding moving arsenals on a defenseless humanity
Abandoned at the mercy of their flag-wrapped carnages.
Countless troops more galvanized to the task than men at work,
Similar to armed carrion-feeders, O senseless pursuits, quenching
Their thirst of blood in the sliced throats of their fellow Men.
Since then, it's been the endless dance of the cowards
Stuffed with titles, nobles devoid of nobleness
Armed, masked, hidden behind human ramparts
Charging against innocents, panicking defenseless populations.
They go about far away lands under hot suns or by serene nights
To provoke envy forcing pity amidst those who only wish to live.
The horsemen of disaster, fomenters of one hundred- year war
Heresy, treason, the massacre of the Huguenots
All false pretexts that haunt human destiny, triumph of non-sense
Killing intelligence, using false pretexts and fallacious proofs
Sacrificing collective pursuits to reinforce selfish personal agendas
Encouraging insolent doctrines by insulting legitimate faith
Nourishing insolent madness by starving genuine goodness
In the name of a God alarmed by mankind's zeal to panic mankind
Rebels, spreading death and sufferings without a justifiable cause
A God that has created us brothers, and enemies to become.
Since Cain and Abel, it's been the endless war cry against freedom

The Hierarchy of Human Sufferings   Ernst
Delma

It's human in exile amidst humankind.
It's mankind killing with bare hands mankind's
Rights to dream, to hope, to live today and to aspire to tomorrow.
One crushes his fellow man by indecent political correctness
For the glory of morally equivocal leaders
Who fantasize and mercilessly crush in turns,
Who pay the executioner's ransom with his victim's blood
Praising a dirty zeal that exalts the crime baseness,
Adorning with silk and gold the horror of the massacre
Enjoying the scornfulness of their haunted souls.
Superb clowns stressing the necessity of bloodshed
For the advancement of inhuman causes.
Since then…it's the slavery of the African race
Thus, in the name of cupidity, debasing the human species.
It's Jews and Arabs rivaling in sardonic horror
Waging wars and apocalyptic terrorist feats,
South Africa and Apartheid, bizarre empire
It's the legality of institutionalized tortures
Iran and Iraq, religious rulers, strange politicians.
It's Central Africa where black-masked specimens
Tear apart each other's heart for incongruous pourboires.
It's Franco, Mussolini, fanaticized militia
The mafia spreading panic in each other's home
For insane, obscure and abjectly aberrant reasons
In the name of wealth, exterminating god.
Since then…it's been the rule of extravagating hatred
Human burns human to pretend human's inferiority
Unjustified treason, vicious crimes by vicious men
In the name of vicious and shallow doctrines.
Shameless riddance of legitimate leaders
Boat people, countless souls resting at the bottom of the ocean
Infernal catastrophes, unwelcome sufferings.
All those offenses committed on every boulevard
In the name of the most senseless logics

The Hierarchy of Human Sufferings   Ernst Delma

To the glory of handicapped theories
Exalting sadly famous Men and bitter doctrines
All those aggressions applied on human by human
That compel humans to regret their humanity.
Every grouchy law-makers, idealistic decision makers
Mixed with inconsistent bourgeois and moody technocrats
Everywhere outlaws make the law and masters of waste reign
Everywhere the carnage against humankind finds a voice,
A favorable terrain for sprouting, and a awkward logic as catalyst
Since then….it's the perpetual and wild savagery
In the name of perverted, shaky, vain and senseless dogmas
Nazism, capitalism, Stalinism, anti-Semitism, nihilism., fetishism
All those devastating, dishonest, unnecessary isms
Having diminished, degraded mankind provoking hardships
All miseries conceived by fiend doctrinarians, makers of debacle
Blossomed, scattered in the field of history
Solemn, passionate, gifted crime crafters
Deadly commotions loyally serving universal terror.
It's been about the human share of the global madness
Since Cain and Abel's ghastly episode.
It's been useless historic guidelines, futile methods
To signify to the Creator the vanity of the Creation
Telling him the pitiful vainness of His divine sympathy.
Fallacious logics legitimizing equivocal pursuits,
Unsuitable maneuvers to enlarge death kingdom
Horrific déjà vu in the wake of Cain/Abel's episode,
The sadly famous of our recurrent man-made agonies.
Since then, it's been an abyss fill of blood and rotten flesh
That no one arrives to define, but one relentlessly refills.
Since then…We've been teaching the Creator a lesson
Compelling him to hide to not pay with his own blood
The mistake of having created us in his image
Downgrading as we evolve from divine to Men
Then to beasts still calling ourselves Men.

As a sustainment to our commitment to elucidate the concept suffering, let's first attempt to agree upon a more or less general definition that would etymologically propose to explicate its unaffected meaning according to the different contexts and texts in which the word might be used. Perhaps its definition will legitimize to the sufferers and to all different concerned entities: divine, familial, religious, and governmental or else that would carry on the necessity of the imposition of suffering-bound retaliations as punishments for some committed aggressions. Having thus done, we would better understand, perhaps, why we are submitted to the rigor of sufferings as an adequate divine retribution for our individualistic and collective misdemeanors.

From the Latin prefix sub and the Latin verb ferre, it would simply mean, to support; but, amidst the different contexts in which it can be employed, the word accepts well a whole wealth of definitions, each one more appropriate than the next or the previous one.

According to the Thesaurus suffering would be: pain, torment, punishment, condemnation, penalty, penitence. According to the Webster, suffering would be nothing else than a certain capacity to accept, tolerate, submit oneself to what hurts us body, spirit and soul.

To better envision it, for the remission of our sins towards God or as a punishment for our mischievous bearings towards our Fellow men or even against our extreme trespassing against societal welfare; we are subject to sufferings going from simple physical pain to atrocious moral torment or to capital punishment.

Would it be redundant to illustrate the arguments of our exposé to call upon all the extraordinary historically fatal spots — that they are biblical or worldly — that have been challenging imagination and have stressed human specie to the extreme limits of human endurance? All those particular events that have slashed with innocent and/or guilty blood(s) the parchment of Universal History deserve indeed a close look upon for the success of our interrogative inquiry.

The Great Flood, Sodom and Gomorra, The One Hundred Years War, The first and second World Wars., the Great Plague, The Pan Am Bombing, Hurricane Katrina, the Asian tsunami, and more recently the chain of deadly earthquakes that of Haiti principally that have made hundreds of thousands of deaths and millions of victims and caused several hundred millions in deficit amidst a nation already impoverished as many — among many more remarkable human catastrophes that have forever and tremendously marked human history in indelible letters and frightening statistics. They are tragic, regrettable, sorrowful episodes, but they confirm, with a high degree of accuracy, human beings' bizarre frictions with insupportable sufferings.

The relationship between anguish and humankind is comparable to an infernal orgy, a gruesome promiscuity, a perfect but imperfect together, a realistic but impossible graft. The lines I am about to submit to your analytic scrutiny more than to your readings humbly sustain the argument that suffering has been with us since the most remote times of human civilization. They will have for virtue to show, tell and prove that humankind has been subjected on this planet earth to a nightmarish experience, an inevitably slow decent into hell with just a few moments of ecstasy, a terrible contrary to all legitimate quests to durably felicitous inclinations and a stubborn deviation to our quest for materialistic, spiritual, physical and moral well-being.

Suffering is — for the least one might be allowed to say — a challenge to the legitimate aspiration to see happier and better moments appear at the horizon of our dreams and of our interests. A sort of fatality devolved upon us no matter what we undertake to circumvent its occurrence or its gravity. Man was born to suffer — must we admit at a certain extent — so much the recurrence of suffering and the relentlessness of whatever provokes it imply the strangeness of its necessity.

In effect, human specie has suffered much and — in all appearances — is inclined to admit the necessity of sufferings in all walks of fashion all along human experience. But, is it true as Alfred de Musset has claimed in his own romantic disorder that "Man is an apprentice, suffering is the master. No one completely fulfills oneself as long as one has not suffered."

Many psychoanalysts, philosophers, gifted scholars, and remarkable men and women of letters have reached the extent to considering suffering and anguish as efficient remedies to humanity's salvation. I mean that our sufferings are born from original sins or provoked by individualistically mischievous factors. Victor Hugo's "every tear washes something" fully illustrates my pretense of plausible explication of the legitimacy of human sufferings.

Suffering would be, if obedience to such a course of idea reveals its necessity, the salutary water of divine provenance that washes our sins, the sacred rag that wipes off the tenacious stains of our offenses towards our fellow men and our iniquities before God. Family, law and divinity support the morally and spiritually constructive inevitability of some sorts of suffering-inflicted punishments.

Matter-of-factly, family through a variety of methods of reprimand, law through sentences going from the supportable to the torturing imposed by our natural judges, divinity through countless natural calamities - sometimes inexplicable in their correlative terror - show no adherence, whatsoever, to our dishonest behaviors. Human institutions and divine entities seem working together, joining forces, to inculcate us good manners through the obligation of submitting us to harsh devices of punishment for the remission of our faults, of our crimes and of our sins.

Suffering cleanses us. Although it sounds, absurd to see in suffering an efficient balm for our spiritual healing, yet a rigorous trajectory towards repentance for our self-inflicted moral pain when having chosen not to be in harmony with the moral principles, emanated from the divine, that govern human kind. There is until the relentless mismanagement of the legal rules that define our social contract to be the cause of personal or collective desperation. Whenever we violate the traits of those pursuits of happiness as defined by the divine or the humane, we suffer as if it was a legitimate and ultimate recourse, a peremptory command from our very essence.

Everything seems to agree to the fact that when we behave, we do not suffer, we share some degree of happiness. On the other hand, through any slight demarcation form, a set f principles that govern men's lives in society, we provoke our own sufferings and those of others. Don't we?

Yes we do indeed; and the strangeness of the situation resides in the certainty that we do not show enough respect to our humanly contract as long as we were not as yet exposed to some kind of painful experience, at times extremely rigorous, which would have for ultimate virtue to form our characters, shape our temperaments and guide our future endeavors. Someone would talk about 'the baptism of fire', and it would be the exact expression to its explication. One must be cast and remolded through suffering - sine qua non condition, it seems - to fully master one's impulsion, to adequately assume one's humanity.

We are destined to suffer, evidently, we must admit. In certain circumstances, we suffer more bitterly than we can bear, beyond our capacity of endurance, and we behave largely better after a good session of unbearably intense sufferings. Proven statistics bear with this remark, demonstrable experience confirm its veracity.

Our suffering is at times so bitter — as for example that observed in the wake of the January 12, 2010 earthquake that has ravaged Haiti and brutally has torn lives out of those more than two hundred thousands Haitians exposed to its rigor - that many intelligent observers, including the German philosopher, Friedrich Nietzsche, the father of Nihilism, questioned God's existence based on the fact of God's manifest absence amidst humankind's sufferings. In his limited although comprehensible examination, he argued that if God existed he would not permit the perpetration, the occurrence and the continuation of whatever is at the basis of those misfortunes that have been plaguing humanity, causing those unbearable sufferings and their merciless hierarchy. His omniscience, omnipresence, and omnipotence should prevail to rid humanity of those fateful manifestations.

As to support Nietzsche's assertion, we enormously suffer, always; and God shines by his apparent deficiency to respond to the call of distress each time. Can we in all liberty, at the risk of being seen as blasphemous, pretend that God deliberately opts to be absent from the premise of the general human catastrophe. That would be another question.

Meanwhile, how do we suffer? Is God really absent when we suffer? The one who promises "I will be always with you until the end. I will never leave you." Can he falter, has he ever faltered? If so, would we ever be able to surmount the difficulties of existence if - even at the very last minute when the pain reveals itself too atrocious to be bearable – he did not interfere even through death to offer deliverance, at times when least expected.

The legend of the man who was walking on the sand illustrates so well God's omnipresence in our moments of distress. But, how do we overcome our incredulity with respect to God's promises and deeds? That would be another question that deserves an ample development.

The previous two questions are rather underlying and add another drop to the vast reservoir of paradoxes concerning the complexity, the complications to the luminous explications to which they give way. The concept suffering then emerges once more in all the strangeness of its implication and/or its manifestation.

God sees sufferings as an absolute requirement for our spiritual formation, a session of humiliation that confers the humility he so proclaims, for our entire growth as Men, as Christians either to repair us to perfection or to make us understand that our mistakes, our misdeeds, all sorts of disobedience to his ordinances are paid in sometimes supreme sufferings as a call, from him, upon drastic measures to get us back on the right track. Don't parents hand sweets out to children, as a way of consolation, after a weeping? Does not the law offer the privilege of a last meal or a last wish before the final execution? Faithfully to God's sentence that we shall earn our daily bread through sweat, don't we get a well-deserved pay-check for our hard work?   Thus, we must expect to look at sufferings; and, truly, we often do not deserve any better than the purge of extreme physical, moral or spiritual sufferings.

This answers the first question. Yes, we suffer. How do we suffer?

We enormously suffer during our terrestrial journey! We suffer in all the integrity and the wholeness of our beings. It simply means that we suffer body and soul. At this point of this exposé, it is peremptory that we define, analyze and provide arguments to the discussion of the three facets of human affliction.

But, first of all, when do we suffer? We suffer all the time, any time, from birth to death, and, sometimes, when the least expected, when we think we don't deserve to suffer. We suffer as we inhale oxygen to feed our organs with the required abundance of fresh and pure air. All stamped that we are by God-pronounced sentence in the wake of our grand-parents' original infractions, suffering is inevitable and is with us to stay. Disobedience to divine laws and lack of respect to the Creator's specific prescriptions have not helped in the perspective of maintaining the good initial relationship with Heaven. Consequently, cleansing - as it is a necessity imposed by God and in proportion to the magnitude and frequency of the offenses - can only be contemplated through anguish.

That we face God's wraths through the manifestation of some implacable natural cataclysm, victimize by our fellow men terror-crafting capability or even by our own willingness to play gods at the detriment of each other, we suffer the same and from birth to death.

Birth itself – as we have previously indicated – is not conceived without sufferings and to render our souls to the Creator while dying is reported - although not measurable or not yet measured - to be one of the most excruciating pains any human being can endure. No moribund has ever been able to utter the magnitude of their pain. In any case, suffering is thus present every minute of our terrestrial experience, and there is nothing as yet to undertake as an attempt neither to delay suffering's failing due nor to defect its eventuality, once the conditions are fulfilled for its ineluctable strike.

The good hope is that there is not just ugliness in the things of life and the good moments, although not plentiful, are many to pretend to being able to balance the infamous inequality, happiness - suffering. We can simply envision suffering with stoicism for having been in the suffering business as long as humanity has been in existence, and we are there to stay. Hence, why not mastering it or curbing our inclination to bring its fury forth?

Any human being in their entirety and their complexity is a triple-sided entity. We have a body, a spirit or mind and a soul. If physiological or biological accident had not deprived us of ant of those parts at birth, we are then one hundred percent functional. To be born in our integrality is a great privilege but makes us inclined to physical, spiritual and moral sufferings as well.

We do indeed suffer:
- Physically
- Spiritually
- Morally

Physical sufferings

The body is the physical component of the human specie. In its definition as in its essence, it would be the privileged temple for suffering, that they are mild or unbearable. In effect, it's on the human body that the effects of suffering are more visible, more severe and more devastating.

At birth, nature exposes us right on the bat to suffering. Leon Tolstoy agrees through his assertion: ***"the newborn's scream at birth is of terror"***, although we have not yet offended anyone except perhaps our mothers for the painful nine months of carrying and nurturing us. No matter how fanciful is Tolstoy's claim; the suffering that accompanies the scream is always palpable. The newborn ugly facial expression is not of happiness as yet, I suppose.

If pain is truly conditional or directly in relation to our propensity to offense, why then a baby, whose soul is not yet tainted by any sin or has not been bodily exposed to any disease-plagued environment, has to experience abominable suffering? What does so urgently, and in all appearances unjustly, implies this anguish prerequisite in everybody's existence? Is it because, as suggests the Bible, that we are the fruits of sin, and that the wage of sin is suffering and death?

Tolstoy's explication, for the least one can say, is impregnated of fallacy and is, for the least, sentimental and subjective. Such a theory, feeble in its essence, would rather make the newborn a nostalgic of the mother's womb, cozy environment, where the little ones swarm about the viscosity of a lovable and tolerant interior, which provides everything from the easy to digest, easy to secrete meals to the beneficial warmth, capable of ensuing survival and growth. Who would elect to leave such an atmosphere for our horrific entourage without expressing the terror of one's soul through a solid unforgettable scream?

True or false, scientifically demonstrable or not, such an assertion implies that the baby receives a hard blow entering a less propitious environment to dwelling and growing. Birth, a natural advent, triggers, consciously or automatically, the familiar piercing scream, that fortunately implies the presence of life in the tiny body, which introduces another explanation this one a bit more convincing because scientific. Our last consideration appears, for the least, susceptible to proof through some sort of laboratory analysis.

Another explanation, more physiological than more probable but does not nevertheless discard the verdict of suffering is that the scream is rather caused by the sudden surge of oxygen entering the body causing a sudden change of atmospheric pressure from the mother womb to the new ambient milieu, causing the partially shrunk organs to abruptly open up for the required pure air intake to travel through the human organism.

No matter how it is perceived and interpreted, the innocent lowing that escapes from the baby's tiny lungs would have for consequence to expose his vital organs to a new world where oxygen is king and command from now on the tiny body's operations. The air thus penetrated by all orifices distributes the tumultuous waves of oxygen meandering through the veins, the muscles and the bloodstream to favor the harmonic functioning of the tiny human being's physical entity.

Also, don't rule out this one, rather prone to fantasy, because improbable and illogical, if ones refers to the retaliation concept, we can conclude that having compelled the mother's suffering, the child suffers as well. Even the bible sustains such a way of thinking. Its prescription:"After having caused suffering, one must suffer in return." - Although pronounced in a dissimilar circumstance – maintains there the concept an eye for an eye. "You provoke suffering, you equally suffer", the Creator would hammer.

Tolstoy's conviction in terms of this theory of suffering introduces as well the idea, by the light of the above argument, that suffering is innate to humankind, that one is believed deserving it or not. The baby is innocent, and yet he suffers and expresses the acuity of his early face to face with the phenomenon 'suffering' in a bitter and desperate fashion. The painful scream similar to the sobs of a wounded baby lamb attests it.

Being born and birthing represent two facets of the paroxysmal commonplaces of physical suffering. A mother that open her nerves, her legs then her mouth to express the extremity of pain in nerves-cracking vociferations is in close encounter with death and does experience deliria, so high is her threshold of suffering.

Sickness, in all its form, makes us suffer physically as well, and at the same time changes our characters. It betters us at every level at the extent of forcing us to morally give up being grouchy or evil-intentioned. There again, the bible does not leave us deprived of supporting arguments.

When Satan to test Job's faith in God advised the latter to submit his servant to a sequel of gradually extreme physical pains and/or materialistic deprivations of all sorts, he really thought that physical sufferings would be the ultimate punishment against which acuity no man can substantially maintain faith. He thought the flimsy character of the servant's faith would be unveiled through the test. On the contrary, Job's already proven faith grew in proportion to his sufferings and has rather aided him to overcome extreme pain. In Job's case, extreme faith against extreme pain is the ultimate determination.

Having unsuccessfully used the physical suffering scheme, Satan – having consulted his vast reservoir of ruse - changed his trick and tempted to discourage Job through moral sufferings. At the prince of darkness's request, God allowed his servant to be the object of temptation through his most precious possessions, his family and his wealth; but, there again Satan's stratagems proved powerless to corrupt the man of God's faith.

Job, having called upon all the resources of his spirituality to overcome the physical, moral and spiritual strengths that overwhelmed him — has never let go on his faith, which has never been compromised, until his natural death set him apart from his family and from his materialistic possessions. He had expired amidst the satisfaction that his faith in his God has never been scratched even when his desperation has reached an insupportable height.

An example, among countless others out of the biblical reservoir, is about a millionaire on his deathbed, affected by cancer. His sickness reached its advanced stage, and his awareness that death was inevitable rendered his pain even more excruciating, for from being simply physical the latter has become moral. In his ultimate moments, just before remitting his soul to the Creator, he uttered to a close one's ear:" If only I could give up 10 millions of my fortune just to live another ten years."

The man in the example has probably made several tens of millions all through his successful career. The cancer that has worn his body and deeply damaged his flesh has - at the same token — provided arguments first to his life's justification, then a testimony to his obtainment of spiritual maturity before his death. He has surely reached that degree of moral and spiritual ripeness through physical suffering, which has helped him at the very last moment to evidence the incontestable fact that money does not quite neither procure genuine happiness nor exempts us from corporal, moral or spiritual pain.

Job has not given up facing the rigor of physical suffering. On the contrary, he had become more and more clung to his spiritual certitude, which helped him overcome his manly weaknesses. His suffering predisposed him to instead harden his conviction. The man in the above example - to worldly illustrate our arguments, him too — has accumulated amidst his corporal sufferings the satisfactory degree of wisdom that has allowed him to transcend beyond the corporal weakness, due to suffering, to reach a certain spiritual fitness at his last breath that propels his soul towards a different dimension. If it was too late for such a swift repentance, God is the ultimate judge; but as far as it concerns humans, his stoical attitude towards his very end showed the late birth in his heart of the ultimate conviction that there is on earth something money cannot buy, health or simple life. He realized last of all, just before entering the vacuum from where one does not come back, that money provides healthcare and lifestyle, not health and life.

The hierarchy of human sufferings proves us no charge is emphasized by the Creator or by Nature. It is in the human nature to suffer. As an inevitable prerequisite to the human existence, one was born, one lives then one suffers. Two examples – essential and simple, but influential and formative, appropriate if one refers to the explication of our true relationship with God and of our true purpose in life when tortured by physical sufferings.

Spiritual Sufferings

The spirit or mind is the intelligible component of a human entity. It is the part that allows Men to lucidly apprehend, comprehend and manage the different circumstances that are fundamental to humankind's daily living. The spirit is the mould of the human intellect. Owing it to the spirit, when well nurtured, well imbued and well-exerted we rule over ourselves, over others and over existence. It is the spirit that rocks the intellect that allows such assertions as that from the French tragedian, Pierre Corneille:" ***I am the master of myself as of the universe; however, I think having no rival whom I harm by treating him as my equal.***"

Although it sounds rather essentially theoretical, we are inclined to believe that spiritually inflicted torture is less violent that the physical one, but we respond better when we react to life circumstances calling upon our spiritual means. Our intellect, when adequately nourished, truly equips us with a higher level of acumen. On the other hand, the spirit - when poorly managed, can transform the human spirit in the temple of predilection where heightened sufferings find itself a comfortable domain and make inestimable ravages on the human soul..

This having said, the mind, when inadequately controlled, can easily become a sponge soaked up with all the dirty waters of existence and consequently more bound to cause us unbearable sufferings, more than the other components (body and soul) are capable of allowing. The more intelligible we are, the more intelligent we become by correlation, the more inclined we are to absorb to satiety all life's regrettable circumstances.

In point of fact, often getting smart transforms our spirit in an ideal conductor of atrocious anguishes. Ironically, we absorb sufferings worse and more poorly manage them when intelligible enough while our intellect should be the most viable weapon to face what life consists of miseries, of misfortunes and of vicissitudes.

Being intelligible and intelligent provides some of us with a high-leveled spirit of justice. As Coriolan Ardouin has, so well, conveyed it:

"All is vanity, pains and miseries
"A just man's heart is a vase of tears."

What he meant was that one just has to possess a keen sense of fairness to become the favorite prey of life and its recurring calamities. In effect, justice, love, wisdom are often concept-traps that have been bringing annoyance, suffering and even premature or commotional death to those who aspire to their enjoyment or to endorse them on behalf of humankind in view to make of the world a better place and of the living a better dream.

Coriolan Ardouin, the prodigiously poetic spirit that has proffered the above quote has perished young for having absorbed the conjugated effect of a series of moral sufferings that have caused in him tremendous internal commotions, then a sentimental collapse resulted entailing the gradual diminishing of his physical endurance. He couldn't bare any longer the physical suffering emanated from a long enduring moral suffering, then the final and fatal fall occurred at age twenty-three from tuberculosis.

His suffering, which was mainly emotional at the very beginning, became spiritual wavering between his enthusiasm to enjoy his young life and the existential catastrophe born from his direct tête-à-tête, one would even talk about a certain misunderstanding, between the man and his existence; and the stronger, the ultimate recourse, death in this perspective, prevailed. The romantic spleen - very in vogue then, and the predisposition from the youth of his age to let the intimacy of their souls be invaded by such an inclination — has not missed to dictate the pace and to inspire to his soul the outpouring of such sorrowful verses.

Immortal verses indeed capable of capsizing anyone's soul in a semblance of shared suffering often wrongly defined as it is at times suitable for the success of some romanticism penchant absorbed by some predisposed souls. The young poet has lived the reality of some sentimental pains that have shaped a particular perception of the things of life, of love and of happiness, feelings proper to romantic spirits.

The exalted imaginations, sensitive to the excess, adopt all that as a fatal vocation espousing fatality as a manufacture of poetic delights.

When incapable to find in emotional ravings the answer to their inner struggles, chose to make peace with life's forces, with God. They enter into harmony with Nature to find an adequate response to their romantic melancholy, a cure even abstract to their somewhat confused souls.

Let's dwell once more for a moment or two in the midst of the bible. Cain — after having harmed to death his younger brother Abel by jealousy because of God's and his own genital father's attention on behalf of the latter — had become tortured by extreme anguish. The famous piece "The Eye of the Conscience", singled out from Victor Hugo's famous poem "The Legend of the Centuries", translates so well the disillusions of his soul coping with his conscience in a duel so fiercely tense that he believed hiding from God's presence would be the ideal solution.

That personal quest having been unachievable, all attempted schemes having been proven inefficient, his suffering became an acute one and swayed between spiritual torment and moral delirium, then dementia resulted; even his inclination to put an end to his life, sentiment that has crossed his mind to penetrate his soul emanated from his moral suffering revealed unrealizable. His suffering had to be complete and slowly redeeming. He had to suffer to the core, indeed, to pay for his heinous crime.

Hence, it is an intrinsic condition to human specie that Man is condemned to suffer a little bit or enormously all along their terrestrial experience. Cain's example compels us to understand that suffering does not always come from the external environment nor is often provoked by some kind of sickness, by God's wrath or by some man-made calamities. Suffering can be an inner experience to not say innate. It is often – and more often than one might think - self-inflicted and directly emanates from the poor management of our relationship with God.

Sometimes, we just have to forsake our own virtues and our own intrinsic values, commit a crime and consequently remove from us that parcel of divinity that God has placed in us at birth that guarantees us the claim that we were created at God's image to make us suffer the most atrocious of all sufferings: moral suffering. To thwart Nietzsche's argument about God's inexistence observed through his remarkable absence to assure the mediation in humankind's self-inflicted dilemmas, someone else whose name slipped off my mind has opined that:"God is not obliged to intervene to punish the perjurer and heaven may stay deafened to human cries, the spiteful individuals possess in themselves the sufficient resources of their own destruction".

Moral suffering is mankind's ultimate affliction and also supreme judge, the one that prevents us from looking ourselves in the mirror or facing our individual or collective conscience. Physical sufferings feed themselves on the body, moral and spiritual sufferings crave on the human soul.

As far as Cain is concerned, his transgression was the apogee of all possible enmities that a man can contemplate, then the extreme expression of suffering became an imperious necessity for the remission of an extreme act of disobedience to the Supreme Being, and — which makes it even worse — emanated from a stand overtly and categorically displayed against God's preference to place his affection where he judged the most appropriate. God has not verbally imposed his wrath for Cain to start suffering. His peremptory:"What have you done?" largely sufficed to unleash hell at the level of Cain's conscience, and hell was indeed unleashed that pierced through Cain's soul from all parts as white-hot needles.

His suffering took a rather tragic bearing, all the more, as all possibilities of expiation appeared existent. Offending God himself through direct confrontation proved to be beyond all degrees of audacity and outweighs human justice; the most famous of all perpetrators known to mankind had to face divine justice. God has openly pronounced his sentence, a sentence with a rather an apparently pacific cachet but a slow process of gnawing at Cain's moral being, an internal distress, one truly ravaging was since then initiated for the guilty one and to the prejudice of humankind.

God has not expressed any extreme urgency for quick punishment pr swift expiation, for Cain lived up to four hundred and twenty-nine years old. But in all verisimilitude, God decided otherwise; and the perpetrator must have inherited an eternal divine retribution. His biblical "Woe to whoever touches Cain" said it all. He has stamped the perpetrator, marked him with the hot iron; his was vengeance, and retribution was his.

Aware of his condemnation to face God's wrath one way or the other, sooner or later, he expressed his desire to hide. But, where to hide from the Supreme Being's omnipresence was the puzzle. How to hide from the one who knows it all, sees it all, and possesses it all? Isn't it written that all is in his hands: out past, our present, our future and even our most secret thoughts, our lives and our belongings? Our catechism lessons told us. He knows perfectly when we are going to sin against his will, but let us sin anyway to better weigh us or explore the depths of our faith.

Could Cain not carry his heinous crime deeply in his conscience? Could he let it slide on his mad nature as dust on a thick block of ice? No, he could not, deprived of such an elevated capacity, as he could not resist the violence of his illegitimate hatred. The burning needles of his mismanaged ambition pierced the softened flesh of his sense of right or wrong. His moral strength, embittered by his hatred, collapsed.

Fighting the raging jolts of his crime, he wanted to flee as far as possible from the offense environment, slip away somehow from the Creator's presence; but to go where or how far from an entity whose dominance goes beyond time and space. To flee from His presence, but where is it in this big Universe that He is not? The Universe is huge but tiny in God's eyes, too tiny to contain God's presence.

Cain could not – in any fashion whatsoever – negotiate with God for the shedding of his brother's blood. God's" The voice of your brother's blood cries unto me from the ground "echoed at the four corner of the perpetrator's conscience. He could not recover the spiritual fullness guaranteed by his creation at the image of God, which he woefully scoffed off. He could not contemplate either any degree of internal serenity; hence the ravage that sat in his conscience, which he could not convincingly control, rendered him demented and delirious.

As narrated within Victor Hugo's epic poem "The Legend of the Centuries", Cain took his family and vainly attempted to hide from God. His mismanaged ire, born from ambition has instilled in him the extreme moral then spiritual disorganization, and he faced harsh torments because he has skilled. His suffering has become not only the principal hitch that has contributed to develop in him a pitiful paranoia; but has also and principally caused the failure of the initial harmony between God and us. The strong material of direct intimacy that the Creator has initiated between him and us having made us in his image has been since then damaged for good and apparently forever.

Morally ravaged by the atrocious character of his aggression, Cain's conscience challenged his crime's magnitude. The greater the offended – not Abel, the victim, himself but God whose degree of affections for the cadet of the two brothers has been the ferment of the fraternal animosity – the greater the offense, not quite the crime itself that was punishable anyway, but the amplitude of the direct disobedience, Cain's bold carelessness to take notice of God's ordinance "Thou shall not kill".

In God's eyes, Cain's was a lot more than an offense with no justification, but an insult with no excuse whatsoever, and even the punishment that would look supreme to humans, death, would look too small and too sweet a punishment. Another sin for which Cain has accumulated extreme culpability in his brother's murder was envy. Consequently, his transgression has met the maximum requirement for God's retaliation, retaliation he has left to his entire discretion when he cried his ultimatum out:" Woe to whoever touches Cain." He wanted no intermediary between in this direct conflict opposing Him to His protégé's assassin

The following verses from Victor Hugo's poem "Conscience" do not miss to remarkably illustrate Cain's dilemma coping with the first most famous crime in the biblical universe as well as in humanity's history.

When, Cain, with his children, clothed in brutes' skins,
Disheveled, livid, rushing through the storms
He fled before Jehovah as night fell
The dark man reached a mount in a great plain
And his tired wife and his sons, out of breath
....
They fled through space and darkness.
Thirty days, he went and thirty nights, nor looked behind;
Pale, silent, watchful, shaking at each sound;
No rest, no sleep, till he attained the strand
Where the sea washes what was Asshur.

Does not the Hierarchy of Human Sufferings find its most powerful expression in this passage? Cain has become an unrepentant perhaps secretly repentant wanderer. His crushed conscience dictated him all sorts of stratagems to pretend to be able to escape God's vindictive gazes, gazes that were rather the ghostly reflections of his tormented soul.

"Let's lie down on the ground and sleep"
Raising his head, in that funeral heaven
He saw and Eye, a great Eye in the night,

Opened and staring at him in the gloom
He woke up in a start.
"I am too near," he said trembling.

No run away approach was good enough: distance, hiding, constructions of a tent, of a wall of bronze, of a vast circle of towers, of a city with a citadel made of brass and iron, the plucking of passersby's and bystanders' eyes, the shooting of arrows to the stars, nothing worked, not even the famous prescription, "let's not let enter God", of the troubled ancestor could not produce the expected effect; and Cain's lamentations out of the abyss of his tormented soul kept spring back up.

"Here pause, hide me, that eye I see it still, that eye is glaring at me ever.", and when he was asked "Oh my Sire, is the eye gone"Nay, it is even there"

Finally he took the final decision, the wiser alternative to his understanding to put an end to his calamity.

"I will live beneath the earth
As a lone man within his sepulcher
I will see nothing; will be seen of none".
But contrarily to his expectations
"The Eye was in the tomb, and fixed on Cain"

Those verses from Victor Hugo typify the example of a man challenging his conscience in a duel that only the conscience can win, never the man. Does not that duel represent an ideal stage for "The inevitable Hierarchy of Human

Sufferings?", the ultimate anguish of a man who could not dominate his passions(s), the fatal surges of his mishandled jealousy.

The promise of eternal beatitude made place, on the contrary, to hideous specter of eternal suffering and even eternal death not only for Cain, but for his progeny, because the original insult to God's heart's penchant was worth us the prospect of eternal damnation. God's free ride of the beginning: unconditional well-being turned into a conditional relationship, and suffering, a whole Hierarchy of those, the sole efficient balm to any pretense to repentance and the possible obtainment of His grace back.

Similar to Cain, when dementia does not tip us in a state of irrecoverable mental disintegration, suffering stays our surer safety valve to proceed to introspective meditation, invite us to conversion and help us to reach that indefectible spiritual fullness propitious to the human elevation towards a desired plateau much closer to the divine sphere where no further damage can gangrene our relationship with each other and with God.

Amidst suffering, when it's not otherwise fatally and irreversibly damaging for the concerned individual, one is virtually on the bench of meditation. All human tragedies, in effect, when not ended in sudden or slow death, replenish the moral and/or spiritual reservoir(s) that ultimately renders us all complete and well-balanced individuals. Based on such a perspective, one can arguably sustain that misfortunes fortunately purge humankind. The Hierarchy of Human Sufferings finds there its raison d'être or underlying principle.

Let us consider once more the biblical legend of the first man created by God to illustrate by another convincing example the origin of the vast and the inexplicable fashions of execution of the Hierarchy of Human Sufferings. Let's consider a moment what Adam's disobedience has cost him in terms of his discarding from Eden and us in terms of tears, sadness, tribulation and all that set human sufferings going and prove us unworthy of the creator's total and unconditional forgiveness.

The" *You will earn your bread through sweat*", he pronounced out of anger, sentence equivalent to" *You are bound to suffering.*" in God's comprehension. One earns his grace since then only on a merit basis. He stopped us from taking his mercy for granted. The felicity, the sweet ecstasy provided by swarming about the Eden Garden has been since then at the horizon of our reach. Even death in itself does not grant us the perspective of eternal life.

Adam has — induced by his companion, herself seduced by the serpent — consumed the forbidden fruit.. It was in the Creator's eyes the kind of disobedience skirting arrogance. Aware of his hitch of divine principles, of his regrettable behavior against heaven's ultimatum, his moral suffering became on the spot unimaginable and insurmountable. His spirituality came out profoundly scratched, nothing could be done henceforth to reconcile him with his Creator, then followed incurable dementia.

Episode that had fatally opened his eyes on his nudity, moral decadence in direct relation with his equivocal bearing followed, which revealed in itself the most atrocious pain inflicted to him as expiation. His conscience turned delirious and spiritual commotion resulted, because his moral blindness committed sacrilege against the sacred.

Adam's exacerbated sense of right and wrong rebelled against the simple but prodigiously efficient verdict pronounced by the Creator. Condemned to sweat much to eat and/or to contemplate even a slight degree of happiness, Adam has learned to suffer in his flesh, in his soul but mostly in his conscience, and − in the midst of suffering - has learned to ruminate over the extent of the sin and the magnitude of the lost. Amidst that moral suffering emanated an atrocious spiritual suffering.

Trapped by his mischief, he spiritually stumbled and disconcertment reached a grave point of no return. For that specific reason − I mean − for the sake of that formation or transformation - whatever appellation the reader would find more convenient − and for the chance to envision once again the perspective of eternal life, is there a ground for all those tremendous human sufferings? More comprehensibly, do there exist means through which the circumventing of the suffering verdict would be possible? Can humankind go back to aspire to the spiritual plenitude God has desired on our behalf at the origin of times?

As far as Adam is concerned, his suffering was more moral then more spiritual than physical. He has indeed suffered in his flesh, but the torture imposed on his soul for having been a hitch to the Creator's devise on humankind behalf tormented him a lot more tremendously.

It would seem, in accordance with the arguments emanated from our previous observations, that suffering is a necessary evil in the perspective that it teaches us first by its very acuity, and then shapes us for better. As a form of surgery, it purges through ridding us of what could damage our health in an irreversible manner. Let's agree with someone that 'what we refuse to learn by wisdom, we learn it through misfortunes'.

One of the most famous names in French Literature, a giant of the Universal Thought, Alfred de Musset, proven romantic for whom suffering is not just as important to the formation of human character as oxygen is for life but is as well a desirable and desired companion, a complicity together painful and essential, once wrote:" A man in an apprentice, suffering is the master." Such an agreement to suffering formative capability illustrates so well the worthwhile characteristics of human sufferings.

Yet, from that inevitable hierarchy in humankind's propensity to and bondage under suffering, which level is more sustainable to another? The suffering, envisaged by Musset, must it be physical, moral and spiritual; and does it teach enough to be the absolute mistress of human soul thus grandly contributing to his formation and transformation we previously mentioned.

In this viewpoint, suffering is our mirror more than a jury. One sees oneself through his suffering than any other mean. One analyzes oneself in the midst of torments, one thoroughly criticizes oneself and one makes oneself aware of what procures happiness as well what causes his anguish in turns.

The basis of Alfred de Musset's moral anguish was his lost love, his forsaken trust and his hurt dignity. Rumor has it that George Sand, his lover, has preferred the famous pianist Chopin to him, which has provoked a slow but severe sentimental breakdown that has catapulted him on the edge of an unsustainable moral anguish, anguish at the least favorable to the success of the prevalent romantic fever back then, the romantic spleen much in demand in the rank of the young poetic minds.

Musset had to accept the evidence of his loss, and in the wake of his deception — strange denouement - he could not rule out his usefulness, which became an accomplice to his exacerbated sentimentalism in search of a rationale for its exteriorization, a painful expectation, the knife of his moral wound and the wound itself, his necessary evil, his inseparable Muse.

Could anyone even in one's wilder imagination see the well-founded of such an implication of suffering as remedy to some sort of thirst for mental drifting? His agreement to his anguish, essential carrier of romantic outpourings, dictated him verses like the following,:" The greatest weal left to me on this earth is to have sometimes lamented." Pure divagations of the imagination aren't they, but that become reason in the unrealistically touched spirits.

The stoic threshold — indispensable — to his own human condition or to the realization of the fullness of his romantic penchant — was reached and his resolute adherence to his sentimental pain has found a rationale in his romantically beneficent raving. Efficient palliative to the, then in vogue, idealistic spleen:" The day the saxhorn will hear my lamentations, my first reaction will be to rave." A strange equation happiness/anguish, anguish/happiness resolved amidst a sweet sentimental violence, propitious to his poetic thirsts of acknowledgement.

Alfred de Vigny, later, suggested contrarily suffering without raving. His stoicism as directly opposed to Musset's penchant to loudly express the sentimental disorder that engrossed his soul suggested suffering and even dying without raving, in other words to accept one's misfortune with certitude. It's when noble endured that suffering elevates humankind before God as before our fellow Men to their full human dignity, as it was the case for the remarkable fortitude displayed by Job in the biblical example as opposed to Cain's dementia.

Another reason to sustain than suffering renders certain persons better, more serene and more superb as it makes certain others viler, more miscreant and more untimely then more vulnerable. It is the case to say that is when facing anguish that one gauges better one's capacities to dignifyingly behave and deserve one's human attributes

In his famous poem: "The Death of the Wolf", Alfred de Vigny has so perfectly brought about such a philosophy of demonstration of moral grandeur in misfortune. The following is such a purely elevating stoicism personified by a wolf.

"To know what one has been on earth and what one has left behind
Only silence is great, everything else is weakness
To lament, to cry, to beg for mercy is all cowardice
Perform energetically your long and heavy duty
In the trade destiny has called upon you

Then, do like me, suffer and die without a murmur."

Seen from all possible angles and analyzed through great details, it appears from the available arguments that suffering cleanses us, brightens our consciences and enlightens our souls. For some of us, it forces us to understand our true mission towards each other and predispose us to see the things of life under better moral or spiritual disposition, to evolve in life armed with a rather grandiose conviction. No matter what the calamities that often overwhelm us make us endure as pain and torments, don't they somewhat render us stoic, in some circumstances more affable or more resolute thereafter to engage ourselves in better, different or more elevated pursuits consequently more justifiable.

Purgatory is a concept of which the true religious meaning escaped totally to the little ones during catechism classes. It leads to an absolute poverty of comprehension to fulfill, which as well is often subject to all sorts of erratic interpretation from grown-ups. It is nothing else than a neutral ground where one learns to meditate on his fate as the result of good deeds or misdeeds. One dwells in Purgatory as a transitory spot to face afterwards the corresponding verdict to doubtful behaviors or to obtain the diadem associated with our decent bearings, our constructive attitudes and predispositions to positively embrace the vast human experience. Suffering is then humankind's purgatory vis-à-vis himself, vis-à-vis others and vis-à-vis God's catechism.

In the wake of terrestrial sufferings, purgatory is the transitory step, the heavenly milieu of hope, a sacred antechamber, which would have the well-defined virtue to give a last chance of repentance, of prevention of the final attachment, of the precocious then fatal weaning, to reroute the trajectory of the of the definitive divorce from the Almighty, to guide our souls through prayer and total self-abandonment to God's care, lastly to help us to truly discover God and to work to deserve his forgiveness and ultimately eternal salvation.

The final phase of human suffering, our absolute surfing board allows us to reach the ideal spiritual fullness and lastly puts eternity at our reach. Thus, we can infer that suffering is salutary. The hierarchy of human sufferings - we must painfully admit - has the ability to deliver us from the yokes of moral and spiritual disorders proper to mankind and propel us towards the dimension where we can contemplate the perspective of a blessed eternity.

In spite of our determination to stay in the biblical context, it is to observe that the cope of our exposé - human sufferings, principally the horrendous cases - requires the reference to recent anguish-causing episodes because of their poignant characteristics, of their occurrences' fundament and the amplitude of the damages they brought about. Their very statistics compel us to see in them palpable examples of ghastly sources of human distress.

Those particular occurrences, fatal for humankind have been dropping our world on its knees and brought about the horrid paroxysm of the Hierarchy of Human Sufferings. It is difficult to attest that those episodes take a defined trajectory in terms of their frequency, their magnitude, their raison d'être, and their destination – which would require us to refer to Nostradamus's predictions. It is to observe, nevertheless, and admit that they were all tremendously, physically, morally and spiritually painful. People exposed to their occurrences have literally suffered in their bodies, their souls and their spirits.

Will the occurrences at the basis of the sad chapters of human sufferings ever stop coming our way? Let's not forget, before all, that nature has its way to manifest its grandeur and its weaknesses. Thus, let's not expect Mother Nature to stop grinding its teeth anytime soon. We will have to face, as long as we are humans, God's wrath manifestations through his most elected medium nature, God's ultimate weapon.

As far as the level of eccentricity we call upon to extract all trace of humanity in our fellow Men is concerned, God would have nothing to do with that. It's simply a bad utilization of the gift he gave us to have dominion on nature through the gift of intelligence that scatters terror.

Also, the Creator has pronounced his timeless sentence, because the Creation has broken the contract through first the original sin, I mean the consumption of the forbidden fruit and then the episode Cain/Abel, the most notorious assassination of all time. To Adam, "Thorns and also thistles shall it bring forth to thee." and further "You will earn your bread at the sweat of thy face." Cain himself carried forth the ultimate symbolic sentences at the basis of human sufferings.

But, let's not rule out our own propensity to provoke our own miseries through and for the very expression of our humanness. Tolstoi's assertion according to which Man carries the worms of his destruction could be interpreted in a more straightforward manner that Man carries in him the sinful enzyme that periodically causes his agony.

"Man is an apprentice, suffering is the master. No one completely fulfills oneself as long as one has not suffered." Then, suffering would be a legitimate expectation, a purifying beatitude; but, in accordance with Alfred de Vigny's stoical perspective, would we ever be able, like Job, to suffer and die without uttering a plaintive accent or like Jeremiah would the expression of grievances wash the sins that constraint us to lament, to cry and to beg for mercy from the Creator or from our fellow Men?

God is not absent, he hides. God is not deaf, he feigns to not hear us to let us face for a moment or two the drama of us, by us and for us. God is not inexistent, we disgust him. The concept of free will comes to play here and should convince us that we are the ones who make the wrong choices at the basis of our distresses. Countless gratuitous massacres on men by men: Religious Wars, World Wars, September 11, the most notorious of the crimes of lese humanity have contributed to dig wider and deeper the ditch between God and us, between Creator and Creation, the Creation having become too manifestly abominable against the Creator's taste.

Let's, as a logical continuum to our expose, look over at least a couple of three harsh episodes that have brought human sufferings to an unbearable paroxysm in their bodies, their souls and their spirits. September 11, the Asian tsunami, the Haitian's subsequent hurricanes and the January 12, 21010 earthquake aren't they of those that physically, morally and spiritually crushed a frightening number of lives.

The following, courtesy of wikipedia.com is a succinct account on some natural cataclysms or man-made summits of human sufferings.

The number of World War I casualties, both military and civilian was over 40 millions — 20 millions dead and

21 millions wounded. This includes 9.7 millions military deaths and about 10 millions civilian deaths. The Entente Powers(also known as the allies) lost more that 5 millions soldiers and the Central powers 4 millions.

The total estimated loss of human lives caused by World War II was roughly 72 million people, making it the deadliest and most destructive war in human history. The civilian toll was around 47 million, including 20 million deaths due to war related famine and disease. The military toll was about 25 million, including the deaths of about 4 million prisoners of war in captivity. The Allies lost approximately 61 million people, and the Axis powers lost 11 million.

2004 - Hurricane Jeanne: casualties 3.035 +

The tsunami 2004;
Casualties" 229,866 2nd deadliest earthquake of all time

2005 - At least 1,836 people lost their lives in Hurricane Katrina and 705 missing.

2008 Sichuan earthquake

Casualties: 69,196 dead, 19th deadliest earthquake of all time" 374,000 injured, 18,379 missing.

Disquieting statistics, truly, those translate the extent of the tacit or deep-rooted insecurity that threatens humankind's happiness.

Conclusively, what words to use to express the horror level humankind experiences when having to cope with such terrible realities? The miserable experience turns out to be even more stinging when it's humankind submitting humankind to such extremely severe anguish. The beyond belief aspect of the fatal occurrence isn't it in itself torment-causing, chill provoking?

In their most painful symptoms, human sufferings are terrifying, how can they be seen and treated as foreseeable? When they are naturally afflicted to humankind somehow emanated from the natural elements, often accompanied by some supernatural connotations – why do we have to rule out such was of thinking – what are the human choices to then prevent, circumvent or simply rebel against the fatal occurrences that cause to lament, to cry, to implore divine mercy or human understanding.

Ultimately, the human specie is condemned to endure all sorts of anguish, to bitterly suffer and with an intensity proportional to the acridity of the kind of misfortunes to which rigor one is submitted. Some of them can indeed cause suffering of the most humanly intolerable. For a convincing example, Haiti was hit by five consecutive hurricanes in one single year and, a few years thereafter, by one of the deadliest earthquakes known to mankind. How much more inhuman human sufferings can get?

That human anguish be self-inflicted, provoked by divine wrath, natural or provoked by the rage of the elements, it has one of three pretensions: ameliorate our relation with God, be in harmony with the Social Contract or to pay for the wrong done to human nature. In this perspective, suffering is a step towards physical, moral or spiritual healing. Hence, when the remedial process does not marvelously work because humankind has shown incapacity to confront suffering and curb its atrocities to one's general amelioration, death or ultimately dementia follows.

Thus, human anguish can be seen as a necessary manifestation. It favors individual perfection or purification, a beneficial subterfuge envisioned by the Creator on behalf of the Creation once we contemplate through suffering the possibility to be in diapason once more with life principles. The sentence pronounced since the origin of the terrestrial experience in the wake of the original sin unleashed a whole wealth of disagreements with the divine ordinances. We are condemned to suffer, and a good provision of wisdom can, in fact, result from even the sharpest sufferings-making incidence.

The Hierarchy of Human Sufferings   Ernst Delma

From the same author:

The Sublime Heights of Generous Passions (2002)

Lasselle (2003)

Dilius et le Pot au Lait (2007)

Verbi Potens Sacra Est (2007)

Les Procès de Dilus (2008)

Et Les Arbres Saignèrent (2009)

Haïti : The Persistence of Misfortune (2010)

Haïti : La Persistance du Malheur (2010)

The Hierarchy of Human Sufferings (2010)

La Hiérarchie des Souffrances Humaines(2010)

Les Passions Dangereuses (2013) (en cinq parties)

De l'Extravagance Musicale à la Gloire Politique : L'Étrange Vadrouille de Michel Joseph Martelly (2013)

From Musical Extravagance to Political Glory : The Strange of Michel Joseph Martelly (2014).

Sòti nan Koudyay Mizik Tonbe nan Gran Panpan Politik: Kalinda Mouche Jozèf Michèl Mateli

The Hierarchy of Human Sufferings   Ernst Delma
(2014).

Amour et Raison: L'appel de L'enfance (2015)

Amour et Raison : L'appel de L'Amour (2015)

September 11 in Images and Words (2015)

11 Septembre en Images et Couleurs(2015)

A Ladder to the Stars (2016)

ISBN : 978098169134

www.ingramcontent.com/pod-product-compliance
Lightning Source LLC
Chambersburg PA
CBHW041128100726
47911CB00002B/73